# Gerry MOUSE

## Charlotte Cooper

### Illustrations By: Raynald Kudemus

To Annika:
I hope you enjoy reading
about Gerry Mouse

Charlotte

To order additional copies of this book, contact:
Xlibris LLC
1-888-795-4274
www.Xlibris.com
Orders@Xlibris.com

# Dedication

This book is dedicated to my husband, who has helped many mice in his life. His love for me has made life a big chunk of cheese!

# Thanks

Thank you to Dora Paige of Xlibris for her guidance and knowledge. And thank you to Steve Hogan for his prolific editorial comments.

Gerry Mouse was a cute little mouse.

Gerry Mouse was brown.

He had white cheeks and whiskers.

Gerry Mouse lived in a huge old building with
many windows. It was called a shelter.

People came to the house all day long.
Gerry Mouse called them humans.

Some humans stayed and stayed. Some kept coming back
again and again. Some were hurt. Some fell down on the
stairs. Some were mean and tried to catch Gerry Mouse.

Gerry Mouse liked to watch human shoes pass his door.

The shoes made different sounds.

Swish, swish.
Squish, squish.
Clomp, clomp.
Clacka, clacka.
Tip, tip, tippy toe.

Gerry Mouse peeked out his door and
saw clumps of snow on the boots.

The humans were stomping their feet and shouting "Brrr!"

Gerry Mouse said it too. It tickled his lips. Brrr.

He said it very slowly. B-r-r-r.

There. That was better.

He pulled on his heavy blue mittens his grandma had knitted.

He pulled on his furry black cap. It
warmed his big mouse ears.

He tied up his big black boots.

Outside, snow was everywhere.

Gerry Mouse made tunnels and slides and mountains.

He played for a long time.

But something was wrong.

Today was his birthday.
And he was all alone.
He was so sad.

Gerry Mouse hurried to the river. He
watched humans skating on the ice. They were
laughing and talking. He was lonesome.

He peered into the reeds by the ice where humans
never look. He saw families of mice skating. They

twirled their tails and jiggled their ears.

Gerry Mouse put his head down and walked
home. He was so sad and so chilly.

# B-r-r-r-r-r.

A big man was sitting on the steps. He said,
"Hi, Gerry Mouse. Why so glum?"

Gerry Mouse shivered. He said, "I am four years old
today.  I lived on a farm with my family, but I was
sent to live with another family. One night I left.  Now
I live here." He said, "I am scared sometimes."

Gerry Mouse went inside. He lay on his tiny bed in front of his little fireplace. A tear fell down his cheek.

He fell asleep and dreamt.

In his dream, he was a big mouse. He was strong and powerful. Everyone called to him for help.

"Gerry Mouse!"

# "GERRY MOUSE!"

Gerry Mouse rubbed his eyes.

He heard Big Man's voice.

"Wake up, Gerry Mouse."

Gerry Mouse heard voices singing.

"Happy birthday to you."

"Happy birthday, Gerry Mouse."

He ran out the door.

Everyone cheered.

The mice were gathered around a big birthday cheesecake. "Have some cake!" they shouted.

Big Man gave Gerry Mouse a bright blue jacket. The jacket matched his mittens perfectly. Four shiny gold buttons closed tightly to protect Gerry Mouse from the cold winter wind. "Four buttons. One for each year of your life!" Big Man shouted.

Gerry Mouse danced in circles so everyone could see his new jacket.

Then he remembered his manners and shouted, "Thank you, everyone. Thank you, friends." A tear came to his eyes, and he smiled a big smile. Gerry Mouse was so happy. He cut big slices of cake for everyone.

Finally, he fell asleep on his tiny bed. He was still wearing his new blue jacket and the blue mittens that matched. He was toasty warm.

Everyone in the big building slept too.

Happy because they had helped Gerry Mouse find happiness on his birthday.

Some had jackets. Some did not.

Some had mittens. Some did not.

Gerry Mouse had both. And many new friends too. Gerry Mouse whispered, "Thank you, Big Man." "Thank you, everyone!"

CPSIA information can be obtained at www.ICGtesting.com
Printed in the USA
LVIW01n0716180516
488536LV00004B/12